BIG BUNNY

Written by Betseygail Rand and Colleen Rand
Illustrated by C.S.W. Rand

TRICYCLE PRESS
BERKELEY

Text copyright © 2011 by Betseygail Rand and Colleen Rand
Illustrations copyright © 2011 by C.S.W. Rand

All rights reserved. Published in the United States by Tricycle Press, an imprint
of Random House Children's Books, a division of Random House, Inc., New York.
www.randomhouse.com/kids

Tricycle Press and the Tricycle Press colophon are registered trademarks of Random House, Inc.

Library of Congress Cataloging-in-Publication Data
Rand, Betseygail.
Big Bunny / written by Betseygail Rand and Colleen Rand ; illustrated by C.S.W. Rand. — 1st ed.
        p. cm.
Summary: Big Bunny cannot paint eggs without breaking them, so very sad, she runs away until the
   other little Easter bunnies think of an important task that is just right for Big Bunny to do.
[1. Size—Fiction. 2. Rabbits—Fiction. 3. Easter eggs—Fiction.] I. Rand, Colleen, 1945- II. Title.
                PZ7.R1523Bi 2011
            [E]—dc22
                            2010018017
            ISBN 978-1-58246-376-6 (hardcover)
            ISBN 978-1-58246-386-5 (Gibraltar lib. bdg)
                Printed in China

                Design by Katy Brown
            The type of this book is set in Fournier.

            1 2 3 4 5 6 – 16 15 14 13 12 11

                    First Edition

This is a story about a bunny.
She was born in the spring along with
all the other Easter bunnies.

Nibbling, poking, and playing, the baby bunnies
grow into little bunnies. One baby bunny . . .

grows and grows and GROWS!

She is Big Bunny.

Big Bunny loves being big.

In summer . . .

the bunnies learn how to
paint eggs and weave baskets.

In autumn, when the leaves turn colors,
the bunnies begin to get ready for Easter.

Big Bunny tries to paint eggs,
but they break when she picks them up.

By mistake, she sits on some baskets.

Big Bunny is sad. She can't seem to do anything right. She hops and hops and hops . . .

and goes far, far away.

The little bunnies cry when she is gone.

They give the signal to form a Bunny Circle.

Their ears touch and noses twitch,
and they know what to do.

They must find Big Bunny and bring her home.

They look and look and look.

Late one starry night, they see a large shadowy shape with long droopy ears and a big puffy tail. They have found Big Bunny!

They all gather into a Bunny Circle.
Their ears touch and noses twitch . . .

and Big Bunny knows the little bunnies' plan.

All winter, the bunnies gather grasses and
weave a giant basket, the size of a boat.

They make a belt and ladders so long that
it takes a team of bunnies to carry them.

In spring, the bunnies lean the gigantic basket against the tallest tree. They sew on the belt and ladders.

The day before Easter, Big Bunny
lifts the enormous basket and
buckles it securely.

The little bunnies fill Big Bunny's basket
with eggs. Then they climb in.

In the night hush . . .

Big Bunny whisks the little bunnies
through farms and towns and cities.

At every stop, the little bunnies tuck eggs into hiding places. Inside each home, children sleep soundly.

When the sun rises on Easter
morning, the bunnies are gone.

Happy and tired, the little bunnies snuggle next to
Big Bunny. They close their eyes and sleep.